Red Alert!

First published in Great Britain in 2007
by Egmont UK Limited, 239 Kensington High Street, London W8 6SA

ISBN 978 1 4052 2934 0
ISBN 1 4052 2934 9
1 3 5 7 9 10 8 6 4 2
Printed in Singapore

One summer's day, Station Officer Steele was talking to his crew. Fireman Sam, Elvis Cridlington and Penny Morris were all on duty at Pontypandy Fire Station.

"This hot summer has left us with a big problem," Station Officer Steele began.

"Yes," smiled Elvis Cridlington. "Dilys's shop has sold out of ice lollies!"

"Not that, Cridlington!" said Steele, pointing to a drawing on the blackboard. "The grass around Pontypandy is as dry as a desert . . ."

"That means it's easy for a fire to start," said Fireman Sam.

"That's right, Sam," replied Steele. "It's very serious. I want you on red alert."

Norman Price and Mandy Flood were out walking along the footpaths of Pontypandy Mountain, They were looking for Woolly, Norman's pet sheep.

"Cor, it ain't half hot," said Norman. "Too warm for Woolly to decide to go walkabout!"

"Let's stop for a rest," said Mandy.

"OK," said Norman. "Tracking Woolly is thirsty work!"

Norman took a bottle out of his rucksack and began to gulp down the fizzy pop inside. "BURP!" he went, when he'd finished drinking.

"Norman!" giggled Mandy.

"Oops, sorry!" said Norman. "Did you want a drink, too?"

"No thanks!" smiled Mandy. "Come on, let's go and find Woolly."

"Follow me!" said Mandy. "I think I heard Woolly bleating over this way."

Norman ran to catch her up. He didn't notice when the empty pop bottle fell out of his rucksack and landed near a patch of very dry grass.

The hot sun began to shine on the glass bottle and before long, a spark appeared, setting the grass on fire!

Dilys Price and Trevor Evans were enjoying a day outdoors, too – bird-watching. They were sitting very quietly in a special hut, so the birds wouldn't know they were there.

"I've seen lots of different types of birds here," said Trevor, as Woolly wandered past. "But I didn't know we were sheep watching, too!"

"BAAA!" went Woolly.

"That's funny," said Trevor. "Wherever Woolly goes . . ."

"Norman is sure to follow! Give me those binoculars," said Dilys.

Dilys peered through the binoculars. "I can't see a thing!" she said.

"You've go them the wrong way round!" Trevor laughed.

Dilys took another look and, sure enough, Norman soon appeared, with Mandy.

"Norman Price!" shrieked Dilys. "What are you up to now?"

"Oh, dear! We came here for a bit of peace and quiet," Trevor muttered to himself.

"Hi, Mam!" Norman shouted, when he saw his mum in the hut. "We didn't know you were hiding in there!"

"Shh! You're frightening the birds away!" said Trevor.

"Sorry, Trevor," called Norman. "Sorry, Mam!"

"Hee, hee," giggled Mandy.

"Come on, Woolly must be somewhere around here," said Norman.

"He went that way – far away!" Trevor shouted after them.

Norman and Mandy walked this way and that, but Woolly was nowhere to be seen.

"Oh, no!" said Norman, after a while. "We've walked in a great big circle!"

Mandy sniffed the air. "Hey, Norman! Can you smell something?" she said.

"Something's burning!" shouted Norman.

They looked over the wall and saw smoke and flames in the dry grass. The fire started by Norman's empty pop bottle was spreading towards the hut. "Look!" said Mandy, pointing.

Trevor and Dilys ran clear of the hut, as it collapsed behind them in a heap. "Just in time!" spluttered Trevor.

Norman knew what to do. "Quick! To the phone box, we've got to get help!"

At Pontypandy Fire Station, Fireman Sam picked up the emergency message.

"Action Stations, everyone! There's a fire by the bird-watching hut," he said.

In seconds flat, Jupiter was heading out of the Fire Station, with Sam, Elvis and Penny in the cab. Jupiter's blue lights were flashing and her siren was wailing.

Nee Nah! Nee Nah!

They had almost reached the fire when, suddenly, there was a loud "**BANG!**" and Jupiter screeched to a halt. A sharp rock in the mountain road had punctured one of Jupiter's tyres!

Fireman Sam was cool and calm. "Elvis, Penny, you change the wheel," he said. "I'll radio for Tom to come with his rescue helicopter."

"Righty-ho, Sam," said Elvis.

When Fireman Sam and the crew didn't arrive, Norman and Mandy began to worry.

"Where are they?" asked Norman. "The fire is spreading!"

Just then, they heard the sound of Tom Thomas's Mountain Rescue helicopter, buzzing in the sky above them.

Norman and Mandy ran near to the fire. "Over here, Tom!" they shouted, waving their arms.

When Tom was in position above the fire, he pulled on a lever. Suddenly, a chute in the rescue helicopter opened and special red water splashed out like a waterfall! The fire went out at once.

But poor Norman was standing too close and got soaked by the red water! "Aargh! Tom, I'm wet through!" he moaned.

"Hee, Hee," chuckled Mandy, from behind a tree. "You look like you've been swimming in tomato soup!"

Moments later, Fireman Sam and the crew arrived. They checked that the fire was out and began to clear away the burnt wood and the glass bottle.

"All safe and sound again!" said Sam.

"Oh dear," said Trevor, looking at what was left of the hut. "I don't think we'll be doing any more bird-watching for a while!"

"It was Norman's pop bottle that caused the fire," Fireman Sam explained.

"It's lucky you arrived so quickly to put it out with your special red water!" Penny told Tom. She looked at Norman, and tried not to laugh. He was soaked in the red liquid from head to toe and looked very sorry for himself.

"Have you learned anything?" Tom asked Norman.

"I'll be really careful not to leave glass bottles lying around in the sun, next time," said Norman. "It could start a fire!"

"And I've learned that you can put out a fire with tomato soup!" laughed Mandy.

"It's lucky we were on red alert!" Fireman Sam chuckled.

Stay Safe!

Can you remember what to do if a fire breaks out?

Get out.
Get the Fire Brigade out.
Stay out!

Sam's Safety Tips

- Never play with matches or lighters.

- If you smell smoke or see fire, tell a grown-up.

- Don't play near hot ovens, or boiling pots and pans.

- Keep toys and clothes away from fires and heaters.

- Ask a grown-up to fit a smoke alarm in your house and test it regularly.